Grandpa's Scroll

Ginger Park *and* Frances Park
illustrated by Kim Dong Hoon

Albert Whitman & Company
Chicago, Illinois

Grandpa is coming to visit this summer.
We've never met, but we're the best of pals.

"Pen pals," my parents explain.

Grandpa lives in a small farming village in Korea.

To see it, I spin my globe and stop it halfway.

That's far. Really far.

Only fourteen hours by plane, he reminds me by letter.
Then I shall see you with my very own eyes for the very first time.

I can't wait! I write back.

We learn a lot about each other through our letters.

I love Popsicles, Grandpa!
I write.

And I love bingsu—
shaved sweet bean ice, Lily!
he writes back.

Grandpa and I write in different languages.
But that's no problem. Mom reads his letters to me.
Later, she rewrites my letters to him in Korean characters.

"They're neat looking," I always say.

Grandpa and I live on the same planet,
but our lives are worlds apart.
I live in a row house in Washington, DC,

while Grandpa lives in a *hanok*—
a village house with a thatched roof.
I walk on sidewalks while Grandpa
walks among rows of rice fields.

I like to paint on my computer screen,

I write to him.

I'll show you how to do it this summer.

We'll have lots of fun, Grandpa.

And I'll show you how to paint Korean characters on rice-paper scrolls, Lily. I'm busy making a special scroll just for you. I paint first thing in the morning at my window while the sun rises over Mount Seoraksan. And I paint last thing in the evening while the moon rises over the same mountaintop. Visions in my head— as are you, he replies.

"What's a scroll?" I wonder.

Dad points to a wall hanging of a wintry scene
and black brushed Korean characters in the living room.
"That's a scroll, Lily."

"Grandpa painted it many years ago," Mom adds.
"The poem beside it speaks of the quiet beauty of winter."

"Did Grandpa write the poem too?"

"Yes, he did," Mom says.

I stare at the scene until it comes alive in my eyes.
I can almost see the snowbirds shivering in the winter night.
I never knew this was called a scroll or that Grandpa
painted it or how beautiful it was.

And now he's painting a special one just for me.

Countdown to Grandpa's visit!

Your scroll is nearly done, Lily. My wish is that we'll finish it together, he expresses in his letter today.

"Finish it together? What does Grandpa mean by that?" I ask Mom.

"We'll see when he gets here," she says.

But the next day, bad news arrives from Korea.

Grandpa died.

Instead of picking up Grandpa at the airport, we board a plane to Korea. My heart feels heavy as the plane takes off.

Fourteen long hours later, the plane touches ground.

We climb into a taxi.

The taxi moves through the quiet countryside.

In his letters, Grandpa told me all about his village.
And here it is, right in front of me.

Gourds growing on straw-thatched roofs.

Eventually, they will all fall down like coconuts,
Grandpa wrote.

Rows of crops where he used to take his walks.

...and think about things, Grandpa wrote.

Tall mountains, and sky.

They make even grown-ups feel like small children,
Grandpa wrote.

Weeping strangers bow their heads at the door of the house where Grandpa lived. The scents of candles and incense in the air remind us that he is gone. Dad nudges me.

"Say hello to everyone, Lily. These are your relatives."

Through their tears, they seem very nice. But I don't know these people. They aren't my pen pals.

That night Mom comes into our room and places a white scroll in my hands.

"This is for you, Lily. I found it with Grandpa's things."

"How do you know it's for me?" I ask her.

"Open it," she says.

Slowly, I unroll the scroll to see a painting of an old man and a little girl walking in the rainfall among tall crops. Balancing an umbrella. Holding hands. Grandpa and me. Like beautiful lace, Korean characters decorate the picture.

My scroll.

"Mom, can you read the poem?"

Mom takes a deep breath, then recites:

Lily,
Young and lovely
Like spring's first blossom.
Raindrops glisten on your petals.

릴리
봄꽃같이 싱그럽고 사랑스러워라
빗방울이 네꽃잎을 토닥거린다

白松

"So Grandpa *did* finish your scroll," Dad says.

"No, he didn't," I say. Something's missing.
"Grandpa's wish was that we would finish it together."

In the morning, I look out Grandpa's window and see what he used to see when he painted.

Mount Seoraksan is so tall. The sky is so clear. But everything feels cloudy.

If Grandpa were alive, we would be home painting pictures on my computer screen right now. He would goof up and we would laugh—together.

I hold up my scroll in the sunshine, wishing Grandpa
were here to help me finish it.

Like rain, words flow out of me.

    Grandpa,
    My pen pal
    Once walked in the rainfall among tall crops.
    Now he walks among the clouds.

Mom guides my hand and together we paint the Korean characters onto the scroll. Afterward, we stare at the painting until the black paint dries.

Once we're home, I'll hang my scroll
right where it belongs—over my bed.
Not my scroll—*our* scroll.
Grandpa's and mine.

Lily,
Young and lovely
Like spring's first blossom.
Raindrops glisten on your petals.

Grandpa,
My pen pal
Once walked in the rainfall among tall crops.
Now he walks among the clouds.

To every grandchild and grandparent in the world—GP

To my dad—FP

For the immigrant generation who misses or wonders about Korean culture
and their children. I hope that you can feel the warmth of the Korean people
and the homeland that you miss.—KDH

Library of Congress Cataloging-in-Publication data is on file with the publisher.
Text copyright © 2023 by Ginger Park and Frances Park
Illustrations copyright © 2023 by Albert Whitman & Company
Illustrations by Kim Dong Hoon
First published in the United States of America in 2023 by Albert Whitman & Company
ISBN 978-0-8075-3020-7 (hardcover)
ISBN 978-0-8075-3021-4 (ebook)
Printed in China
10 9 8 7 6 5 4 3 2 1 WKT 26 25 24 23 22
Design by Rick DeMonico

For more information about Albert Whitman & Company,
visit our website at www.albertwhitman.com.